THOR

BLOOMSBURY EDUCATION
Bloomsbury Publishing Plc
50 Bedford Square, London, WC1B 3DP, UK

BLOOMSBURY, BLOOMSBURY EDUCATION and the Diana logo
are trademarks of Bloomsbury Publishing Plc

First published in 2020 by Bloomsbury Publishing Plc

A catalogue record for this book is available from the British Library

ISBN: PB: 978-1-4729-7113-5
ePDF: 978-1-4729-7114-2 ePUB: 978-1-4729-7116-6

2 4 6 8 10 9 7 5 3 1

Typeset by Integra Software Services Pvt. Ltd.

Printed and bound in China by Leo Paper Products, Heshan Guangdong

All papers used by Bloomsbury Publishing Plc are natural, recyclable products from wood grown in well managed forests and other sources. The manufacturing processes conform to the environmental regulations of the country of origin

Catch Up is a charity which aims to address the problem of underachievement that has its roots in literacy and numeracy difficulties.

To find out more about our authors and books visit www.bloomsbury.com and sign up for our newsletters

BENJAMIN HULME-CROSS

Illustrated by
Alessia Trunfio

BLOOMSBURY EDUCATION
LONDON OXFORD NEW YORK NEW DELHI SYDNEY

CONTENTS

Thor and the Frost Giant

Thor was a Norse god. When he was angry he would make thunder boom and lightning flash. His weapon was his great hammer.

Thor loved his hammer. No one was allowed to touch it. The hammer was magical. It could bring dead things back to life.

Loki was a Norse god who liked to play tricks on everyone.

Thor and Loki lived in Asgard, the land of the Norse gods.

One day Thor woke up. His hammer had gone!

"WHERE IS MY HAMMER?" shouted Thor. "WHO HAS DARED TO TAKE MY HAMMER? I WILL KILL HIM!"

Thor was in a temper. He made thunder boom and lightning flash.

Loki looked at Thor and laughed. He was used to Thor's bad temper.

"Where did you last see it, Thor?" asked Loki. "Have you looked under your bed?"

"Of course I have," said Thor. "That's where I always put my hammer when I go to sleep. Someone has taken it!" He said to Loki, "Is this one of your tricks?"

"No, no, no!" said Loki quickly. He liked playing tricks on Thor, but only someone with a death wish would take Thor's hammer.

"I tell you what," said Loki, "you keep looking in Asgard and I will fly off and see what I can find out."

"And when I find out who has taken my hammer," said Thor, "I will bash his brains out."

“Nice,” said Loki. Then he put on his wings and flew out of the hall.

Loki had a good idea who had taken Thor's hammer. He thought it might be Thrim, the king of the frost giants. Thrim had always wanted to be king of Asgard, and for that he needed Thor's hammer.

Loki flew north to look for Thrim. As Loki flew further north, the air grew colder and colder. It was so cold that Loki's beard became a block of ice! At last Loki found Thrim.

Thrim was sitting on a rock. He had white eyes and blue hair. Next to him on the rock was his pet dragon. When the dragon saw Loki in the air, he gave a great roar and a ball of fire shot out of his mouth.

"Keep your dragon away from me," shouted Loki as he flew down and landed in front of Thrim.

"Loki!" cried Thrim, "it is good to see you! I know why you are here. I think I have something you want."

"Where is Thor's hammer?" asked Loki. "I know that you have got it! Nobody else would dare to take Thor's hammer."

Thrim pointed at the icy ground.

"It's a few miles down there," he laughed.

Loki did not know what to do. If Thrim had used his magic to hide the hammer deep underground, nobody would be able to find it.

"But you don't need to look so sad," said Thrim. "I will give it back."

"Really?" said Loki, "will you really?"

"Of course I will." The giant had a big smile on his face.

"All I need you to do is to send me Thor's sister, Freya. I want to marry her. If she will be my wife, Thor can have his hammer back."

"Freya will never agree to that," said Loki.

Thrim laughed and laughed.

"Then Thor will never see his hammer again," he said. "I will become king of Asgard and kill Thor with his own hammer."

***

Loki flew back to Thor. He told him that Thrim had stolen the hammer. When Thor heard this, he was very angry. He made thunder boom and lightning rip through the sky.

"How dare he take my hammer?" shouted Thor. "I will get it back and bash his brains out." But Loki told Thor that Thrim had said he could have his hammer back if Freya became Thrim's wife.

"MY SISTER WILL NEVER MARRY THRIM," said Thor. "SHE IS A GODDESS. He is an ugly frost giant!"

"You would get your hammer back," said Loki.

"That's true," said Thor.

So Thor told Freya about Thrim's plan.

"Don't even think about it," said Freya. "I will never marry Thrim. I am a goddess and he is an ugly frost giant. And anyway, I can't stand the cold."

Thor, Loki and Freya were silent for a while. Then Loki began to smile.

"I've got an idea..."

When Thor heard what Loki's idea was, he was very cross.

"I WON'T DRESS UP AS A WOMAN!" he yelled. "I DON'T TRICK PEOPLE, I FIGHT THEM!"

"Do you want your hammer back or not?" said Loki. "If you do want it back then you will have to pretend that you are Freya. I will take you to Thrim. He will give your hammer back and then it's up to you. You can kill him or..."

"OR WHAT?" Thor cried.

"Or you can marry a frost giant!" laughed Loki. Thor's eyes flashed red and he sprang towards Loki, knocking over a few tables on the way. Loki ran to hide.

"You would get your hammer back," said Freya. "After all, we look alike. My hair is red and so is yours."

"But I have a fine red beard," said Thor, "and you have no beard at all."

"That's true," said Freya, "so you must shave off your beard."

"Well," thought Thor, "I suppose it makes sense. Of course, the disguise will have to be good."

"We will make you a wedding dress and a beautiful veil so that Thrim cannot see your face," said Freya's servants.

"I will give you one of my necklaces," said Freya. "Then you will look more like me."

"We will spray you with perfume. That will make you smell more like a lady," said Loki.

"Well, I have an idea too," said Thor. "If I have to dress up as a bride to get my hammer back then you must be my bridesmaid and come with me."

"Oh no!" said Loki.

The very next day, Thor and Loki set off on their journey to the land of the frost giants.

Thor was dressed as a bride. Loki was dressed as a bridesmaid. They wore veils to hide their faces.

***

King Thrim was very excited.

"Did you see the lightning last night?" he said to the other frost giants. "That must have been Thor putting on a show for Freya for her wedding day!"

Just then there was a loud knock at the door. Thrim opened it. Thor stood in the doorway, hidden behind his veil. He was wearing Freya's necklace and he smelled very nice.

"You must be Freya!" said Thrim happily. "How beautiful you look and what a powerful knock you have. And you have got your lovely bridesmaid with you." Thrim looked at Loki but he did not recognise him behind his veil.

"My dear," said Thrim, "you must be freezing. "Come in, and have something to eat."

The bride and the bridesmaid sat down at the table. The table was full of delicious food for the wedding. Thor was starving after the journey, so he began to eat and eat. He ate a whole cow, six big fish, four loaves of bread and ten cakes. Soon he had eaten all the food on the table.

Thrim was surprised. "I am pleased that my bride likes her food so much," he said.

Quickly Loki thought of an answer. "Freya has been so excited about the wedding that she has not eaten for days," he said.

Thrim lifted up Thor's veil. "I must kiss my bride-to-be," he said.

When he saw Thor's eyes, he got a shock. Thor was so angry his eyes were blazing red.

"Why are her eyes so red?" asked Thrim.

Quickly Loki thought of an answer. "She is so in love with you that she has not been able to sleep for a week," said Loki.

"My beautiful bride's eyes are burning with love for me," said Thrim. "We must be married at once. Bring me Thor's hammer! I will send it back to him."

One of the giants left the hall and came back with the hammer. He put it in front of Thrim.

As soon as the giant let go of the hammer, Thor sprang to his feet. He ripped the veil from his head and grabbed his hammer.

"I AM THOR, GOD OF THUNDER AND LIGHTNING, AND NO ONE WILL HAVE MY HAMMER!" he cried. Then he waved the hammer above his head and brought it down on Thrim's

skull. Thrim's brains sprayed the walls of the ice palace. Next Thor ran around the hall. One by one he struck the frost giants with his mighty hammer. One by one they fell to the floor with smashed bones and broken necks.

When Thor stopped all the giants lay dead on the floor.

"Thor!" said Loki. "What a mess you have made of your lovely wedding dress!"

"I will make a mess of you!" said Thor and he chased Loki all the way back to Asgard.

The Serpent of Midgard

"I'M THIRSTY!" Thor shouted. "AND WE HAVE RUN OUT OF BEER!"

"Well, do something about it," said Loki.

"Why don't you go and ask the god of the sea to make some more?"

"OK, I will," said Thor. "I need some beer." His throat was dry. He ran down to the shore and dived into the sea. Then he swam down to the cave where the god of the sea lived.

"Do you want beer for all the gods in Asgard?" said the god of the sea. "Then you must bring me a big cauldron to put it in."

"OK, I will," said Thor. His throat was drier than ever.

He swam back to land and disguised himself as a man. He put his hammer on the ground and left it there. He knew he would need both hands to carry the cauldron.

Then he set off to find the giant called Himm. Thor was sure he would have a cauldron that was big enough.

***

Thor arrived at Himm's huge hall and knocked loudly on the door. Lora, the giant's wife, let him in. She took one look at his red hair, his beard and his big muscles. She was not fooled by his disguise.

"I know who you are," she said. "Himm always said that one day the gods would come for his cauldron. I hope you take it. The silly thing takes up far too much room!

"Quick, you must hide before he gets home. He won't be happy to see you."

Thor looked around the hall. At one end of it the cauldron lay upside down. It was so big he could hide under it.

"Think of all the beer we can fit in that!" he said. "But for now, it can be my hiding place."

He lifted the edge of the cauldron off the floor and crawled underneath.

As soon as he was hidden, Thor felt the ground shake as Himm the giant came into the hall. Lora asked Himm how his day had been and poured him a drink. Then she told him that they had a guest.

"Where is he?" asked Himm. He didn't sound very pleased.

"Under the cauldron," Lora said. Thor began to wonder whether he had been tricked. A moment later Himm hit the side of the cauldron with his big fist. It made a loud CLANG.

"COME OUT!" Himm cried. Thor did as he was told.

Himm looked at Thor but he did not recognise him as a god.

"You can stay the night," said Himm. He didn't like it. But he knew he should look after a guest.

That night Thor lay awake for hours. He tried to think of a way to steal the cauldron. He couldn't kill the giant because he didn't have his hammer. He couldn't sneak off with the cauldron in the night because it would make too much noise. He would have to try and find a way to get the giant to hand it over. At least Lora did not want the cauldron and would be glad to get rid of it, thought Thor. Then he fell asleep.

The next morning Himm woke Thor up.

"We have run out of food," he said. "If you're staying another night you will have to come fishing with me. Go outside and get some ox poo. We can use it as bait."

Thor was angry. "A god like me should not have to pick up poo!" he said under his breath. So he went outside and found the biggest ox in the field.

"That will make good bait for fishing," he said. He grabbed the ox by the horns and ripped its head right off!

The head was dripping with blood as Thor carried it down to the beach. Its dead eyes stared at Thor.

When Himm saw Thor carrying the ox's head he was very angry.

"How dare you?" said Himm. "You have ripped off the head of my best ox. You must pay for it. If you don't catch enough fish to feed us for a month, we will eat you!"

"Well, let's get out to sea," said Thor. He threw the ox's head into the boat, then he climbed in and grabbed the oars.

Himm almost fell out of the boat as Thor pulled on the oars.

"You're stronger than any other man I have ever met," said Himm with a frown.

The huge boat rocked from side to side as the waves grew bigger.

"That's far enough," said Himm. But Thor carried on rowing. Harder and harder he pulled on the oars. Faster and faster the boat sped across the waves.

"You're not a man," said Himm. Thor just smiled.

"Let's go fishing," he said. "This far out we should catch something fit for a giant and a god."

Himm cast his fishing line into the sea while Thor began to tie the ox's head onto his own fishing line.

Himm pulled in his first catch. It was a whale! The boat rocked as the giant pulled it onto the deck.

Thor was still fixing the ox head on to his own fishing line. Himm fished another whale out of the sea and landed it in the boat. Finally, Thor was ready.

"This should get us something big," said Thor as the ox's head sank beneath the waves.

Deep down at the bottom of the sea, the great serpent of Midgard was sleeping. The serpent was huge. It could not see the end of its own tail.

So, it tucked its long tail into its mouth so that no one could attack it. Now the serpent opened its eyes. It could smell ox blood. Slowly it slid its tail out of its mouth. Its nose could sniff where the smell of the blood was coming from. Then it shot through the sea like an arrow and clamped its jaws around the ox's head.

In the boat, Thor's fishing line suddenly pulled tight. The boat sagged down lower in the sea. Thor held on to the fishing line.

"Let go! It is too big," Himm cried. "We're going to sink!"

"NEVER!" Thor shouted. He put both feet in the bottom of the boat, bent his knees, and began to pull in the fishing line.

The boat sank lower still and waves began to spill over the edges and into the boat.

Thor gave a great shout, "I AM THOR, GOD OF THUNDER AND LIGHTNING, AND I WILL NEVER GIVE UP!"

Himm looked scared. Now he knew he was sharing his boat with the great god Thor. Then the serpent's head came above the waves. Its teeth were still clamped shut round the ox's head. Thor and Himm watched as the ox's head slowly slipped down the serpent's throat. The fishing line was still fixed to the ox's head.

"LET GO of the fishing line!" Himm screamed. "Or the serpent will pull us under the water."

"I'm not giving up," said Thor. "I'm going to catch this serpent."

Just then, Thor's feet broke through the bottom of the boat. The boat was sinking. They were going to drown or be eaten by the serpent. Himm grabbed a knife and cut the fishing line. The serpent gave a loud hiss and sank back down to the bottom of the sea.

Thor was very angry.

"I had to cut the fishing line!" said Himm. "We would have drowned."

***

It took a long time to row back to shore with two whales on board and two holes in the bottom of the boat. Thor and Himm did not speak to each other. Himm was working things out. "Why has the god Thor come to see me?" he thought. "I bet he came to get my cauldron." Himm had always known the gods would try and steal his cauldron because it was the biggest cauldron in the world.

Himm began to think of a plan to stop Thor getting his cauldron.

When they got back to the hall, Lora was amazed to see they had caught two whales.

"You must both be even stronger than I thought," she said. "Himm, maybe we should give Thor your cauldron, to say thank you for his help."

Himm had a sneaky look in his eye.

"Sometimes people are not as strong as they seem," said the giant. He picked up a glass goblet. "If Thor is strong enough to smash this goblet then he is strong enough to carry the cauldron. All he has to do is break this glass goblet. Then he can have my cauldron."

And that is what Thor did. He threw the goblet hard at Himm. The goblet hit the giant between the eyes and smashed into tiny splinters.

Without another word, Thor lifted the cauldron onto his shoulders and marched out of the hall. Himm was very, very angry but he knew he had been beaten. Lora was happy. She looked at all the extra space she had in the hall now that the cauldron was gone.

Thor took the cauldron to the god of the sea who filled it with beer. Then Thor returned to Asgard, and the gods had enough beer to drink for many years.

Thor's Big Adventure

Thor was bored.

"I want a new adventure," he said.

"I had better come with you," said Loki. "You will only get into trouble without me."

Thor and Loki climbed into Thor's chariot. Thor took his magical hammer with him. The chariot was pulled by two huge goats. Thor and Loki set off to find the giant king's hall.

In the evening they came to a small farm. "You can stay here," said the farmer. "But we only have thin soup to eat." Thor was very hungry.

"Why don't we eat the goats?" said Loki.

"Good idea," said Thor. "But you must be sure to not snap any of the bones."

The farmer's children did not hear Thor's warning about the bones. When they ate their meal that night, Ros, the farmer's daughter, ate carefully. But as her brother Alf pulled the meat off the bone, one of the bones cracked.

The next morning Thor held his magical hammer over the goats' bones. It brought the animals back to life. But Thor saw that one of the goats had a bad leg.

"Who broke my goat's bone?" he roared. "Now we cannot go in my chariot. We must walk!"

Alf put up his hand. "It was me," he said.

Thor lifted up his hammer. He was going to bring it crashing down on Alf's head.

"Stop," said Loki quickly. "Why don't we take Ros and Alf with us? They can be our servants."

"OK," said Thor.

"Where are we going?" asked Ros.

"To the giant king's hall," said Loki. "That should be fun, shouldn't it?"

Ros and Alf shook their heads. They looked pale and scared.

***

After walking all day, they came to a big cave. They made a fire, ate some food and went to sleep.

When Thor woke up, he looked out of the cave. There was a giant lying asleep outside.

Thor grabbed his hammer and marched out of the cave. The giant sat up.

"Oh!" said the giant with a yawn. "We don't see many tiny people around here. You must have slept in my glove last night. Was it comfortable?"

Then Loki, Ros, Alf and Thor watched as the giant fitted his huge hand into the cave.

Thor did not like being called tiny. He was a mighty god.

"Where are you going?" the giant asked.

"We are off to see the giant king," said Loki.

"Well, be careful," said the giant. "The king really doesn't like little tiny people like you."

"Who are you anyway?" asked Thor.

"I'm Skrim," said the giant. "I'm going to see the giant king too. We can travel together."

They walked all day and by the evening they were very tired. They ate a quick meal and fell fast asleep.

Then Skrim began to snore. It was a very loud snore.

Thor woke up in a temper. He grabbed his hammer and went over to the giant.

"First you call me tiny, then you wake me up. I will kill you!" said Thor.

Thor lifted up his hammer and hit the giant's head as hard as he could.

Skrim opened one eye.

"What was that?" he asked. "Was it a leaf falling on my head?"

Then he went back to sleep. Soon he was snoring again.

Thor lifted up his hammer again. He brought it down on the giant's head as hard as he could.

Skrim turned over in his sleep.

"Shoo, fly," he said and he waved his hand around.

The third time Thor hit Skrim, the hammer got stuck in Skrim's skull.

Thor pulled the hammer out quickly.

"Is that rain dripping on my head?" said Skrim. Then he saw Thor standing by him. "Hello Thor," he said. "You should try to get some sleep."

Thor was very, very angry. Everyone was afraid of his hammer. His hammer killed anything it touched. And now it wasn't working!

The next morning, Skrim wasn't there.

"Good!" said Thor. "I never want to see him again!"

"Look," said Ros, "here are three huge holes. Where did they come from?"

"I have no idea," said Loki.

At last they reached the top of a hill. Ahead of them they could see a great hall.

"This must be where the giant king lives," said Thor.

Thor gave the door a bash with his hammer. It swung open.

The hall was full of giants. There were giants sleeping on giant benches and giants eating out of giant cauldrons. And at the far end of the hall sat the biggest giant of all with a giant gold chain around his neck.

"He must be the king," said Loki.

Alf and Ros were scared. The giants turned to see who had broken into their hall.

"That isn't Thor, is it?" said one giant.

"It can't be," said another giant. "He's too small!"

"He is so small we could throw him out," said a third giant.

"Or we could eat him," said another giant.

"WELCOME!" roared the giant king. "You have red hair. You have a red beard. You have a big hammer. You must be Thor," said the king of the giants. "But I thought Thor was big, and you look so small."

Thor was shaking with anger.

"Well, I can drink more than any giant here!" said Thor.

"Oh no!" thought Loki. "This is a bad idea."

"OK," said the giant king. He clapped his hands and a giant brought him a huge drinking horn. It was bigger than Thor. It was full of beer.

Thor grabbed the horn and drank and drank. He was sure he could empty it in one go.

But no matter how much he drank, he couldn't finish it.

"Dear me!" said the giant king. "You're not very good at this are you? Still, you are rather small."

Thor threw the horn onto the floor. "Who cares about drinking?" he shouted. "I am the mighty Thor. I'm stronger than the strongest giant here!"

"This is a really bad idea," said Loki.

“I know,” said the giant king. “I have an easy test for you. Can you lift my cat?”

Thor’s eyes burned red.

“Of course I can lift your cat. I am Thor, god of thunder and lightning,” he said.

But when he saw the cat, Thor changed his mind. It was huge!

Thor could stand up underneath it. The cat hissed in his face.

Thor reached up and poked the cat's belly.

The cat arched its back. Thor tried again. He stood on tiptoe and poked the cat again. The cat lifted one paw off the ground.

"It's too big! It is not fair!" shouted Thor. The giants laughed so hard that two of them fell off their benches.

"I'm sorry Thor," laughed the giant king. "I should never have asked a titch like you to lift my cat."

"Titch? TITCH? TITCH!!!" shouted Thor so loudly that the roof of the giants' hall shook. "I will fight anyone here. Then you will all see I am no titch!"

The giant king agreed. "Well, you can fight with Elli. She's the oldest person here. But she can beat everyone."

"Not me," said Thor. "I am a mighty god. I can win easily."

Elli limped over to Thor. She was leaning on a stick. She waved at Thor.

"Is this the titch?" she asked.

Thor lost his temper. "I am Thor, the god of thunder and lightning. No one can beat me!" he yelled.

He ran towards Elli and crashed into her. She didn't move an inch.

He grabbed her by the shoulders and tried to throw her – but she did not move.

Then the old woman took Thor's hand. She gave it a little twist. Before Thor could blink he was down on one knee. Elli held his arm and twisted it behind his back. The giants laughed and cheered.

"Stop!" said the giant king. "We have seen that there is nothing you can do. Now we must eat and then go to sleep."

The next morning, Thor wanted to leave before anyone else was up. He woke up Loki and the children. Then they all crept out of the hall.

"Stop!" said the giant king, who was waiting for them outside. "Did you enjoy your stay with me?"

"No," said Thor. "I'm glad I came because nobody else has ever been brave enough to come here. But I hate losing."

"Don't be so hard on yourself." The giant king smiled. "I won because I used magic."

"What do you mean?" asked Thor.

"Skrim, the giant you met… that was me in disguise. Each time you hit me with the hammer you would have killed me without my magic. But I used a spell to protect my head. Do you remember those three big holes in the hill? They were made by your hammer when you hit my head."

"And what about the other tests?" asked Loki.

"My magic put the end of the drinking horn in the sea," said the giant. "Nobody can empty the sea."

"What about the cat?" asked Alf.

"The cat was really the great serpent of Midgard. Nobody can lift the great serpent."

"What about the old lady?" asked Ros.

"She was old age itself. Nobody can defeat old age."

Loki laughed. But Thor shook with anger.

He raised his hammer and swung with all his strength at the giant king's head. But the hammer cut through thin air. The giant king had vanished.

Thor did not speak all the way back to Asgard.

"What will everyone say about me?" asked Thor.

Loki didn't want to upset Thor. "They will say that there is no challenge that Thor won't try," said Loki.

"Well, that's true," said Thor and he smiled.

Bonus Bits!

Guess Who?

Each piece of information is about a character from one of the stories. Can you match them up? You can check your answers at the end of the book.

1 Thrim

2 Alf

3 Loki

4 Elli

5 Thor

6 Skrim

7 Himm

8 Freya

A there is no challenge he won't try

B dressed as a bridesmaid

C king of the frost giants

D Thor's sister

E caught two whales when fishing

F broke one of the goat's bones when eating

G the giant king in disguise

H the oldest giant in the hall

Norse Mythology

Thor, Loki and the other characters in this story are from Norse mythology which is a collection of stories and beliefs people had in Scandinavia and other parts of northern Europe in the time of the Vikings.

What Next?

- Which of these stories do you like best and why?
- What do you learn about the character of Thor during these stories? What are his strengths and weaknesses?
- Why not try writing your own story about Thor – think about an adventure he could go on and what might happen. There are other Norse gods and goddesses – find out who these are and then choose one or two to be in your story.

ANSWERS TO GUESS WHO

1C, 2F, 3B, 4H, 5A, 6G, 7E, 8D